Thank you!

My first special thank you is to Darlene and Dorian Dybas; without them and their publication, *Coffee News*, this book would never have been published. Next, I would like to thank MargaretAnn Cross and James Van Fleteren for their creative guidance. I would also like to offer my warm appreciation to Sandy and Jim Kukalis for their help and belief in me and this project.

I would like to extend an extra special thank you to my niece, Elizabeth, who will always have a special place in my heart, and my husband, Dan, for his support, encouragement and unfaltering belief that it could be done and that I could do it – I love you.

I dedicate this book to my husband, Dan,
and to my six children: Danielle, Sarah, Andrew,
Matthew, Abigail and Libbey.

You are all God's greatest gifts to me.

God's Greatest Gift

Written and illustrated by

Deborah Burch

Is God's greatest gift

the stars in the sky,

or the sun and the moon so high?

Is God's greatest gift

the mountains and the plains,

Is God's greatest gift

the creatures that swim *in* the sea,

or the

animals that roam free?

Is God's greatest gift

the teeny, tiny bugs

or the

hot chocolate *in your mug?

Is God's greatest gift

the beauty of this place,

or the smile *on your face?

All these gifts
are precious, it's true,

but God's greatest gift is

YOU!

All gifts come from heaven—
so go back and look for gifts of seven.
See if you can find seven of one item on each
illustration.

For the answers, visit www.godsgreatestgift.net.

© Robin Scully Photography

About the Author

When Deb Burch first had a dream about creating a book that would remind children
how much God loves them, she looked heavenward and asked, "Really? This, too?"

Raising her children and working full-time for an artist, Deb felt grateful for the inspiration,
but she believed she was too busy to do anything else. Her life, however, has been a series of small miracles,
so she knew that, somehow, creating this book was her responsibility.
Several years later, she completed the illustrations during the 40 days of Lent.

This time, on Easter Sunday, when she looked to heaven, it was to say, "We did it."

Deb Burch is a graduate of Kendall College of Art and Design.
She lives with her husband, Dan, and six of God's greatest gifts in Manchester, Michigan.

Resources

Design and Typesetting
The Van Fleteren Group I www.vanfleterengroup.com
David LaBre Allen | davidlabreallen.com

Digital Services
Kolossos Printing Inc. | www.kolossosprinting.com

Scrapbooking paper products
Daisyd's © | www.daisydpaper.com
Crafts, Etc! © | www.craftsetc.com
My Mind's Eye © | www.mymindseye.com
Junkitz © | www.junkitz.com
Paper Adventures © | www.anwcrestwood.com/pahome.html

To order additional copies of God's Greatest Gift,
and other books by Deborah Burch, please visit
www.godsgreatestgift.net

God's Greatest Gift, LLC

P.O. Box 185
Manchester, MI 48158
godsgreatestgift@comcast.net